## Binsy Boban Amal

Binsy Boban Amal is an emerging author from the picturesque village of Wayanad, Kerala. Growing up in a home where books were cherished, she was profoundly influenced by her father's love for reading, which ignited her own passion for storytelling. Her writing beautifully reflects her rich cultural heritage and explores the deep connections between the past and present.

After her marriage, Binsy joined an ancestral family in Vadavucode, who wholeheartedly supported her love for books. In her spare time, she enjoys spending time with her family, exploring new cultures, and immersing herself in books and stories that celebrate diverse traditions. With each word she writes, Binsy aims to weave her experiences into narratives that resonate with readers.

English Language
My Little Pumpkins
The Love of Siblings
(Stories)
by
Binsy Boban Amal

♦

Published in October 2024
by Kairali Books Private Limited
Thalikkavu Road, Kannur.
Ph : 0497-2761200
E-Mail : kairalibooksknr@gmail.com

♦

Illustrations
Ravina Sunil

♦

Cover Design
Prasanth Mangad

♦



73/24-25/Sl.No.1640/200/NS.18.6
ISBN 978-93-5973-630-3

# My Little Pumpkins
## *The Love of Siblings*

**Binsy Boban Amal**

Kairali Books

To my dad - Who taught me to read.
To my mom - Who struggled to raise us.
To my father-in law- Who always encourages me to read
To my husband - my greatest support.
And to our family …

This book is for my little readers and Mommies. I have two little kids like you, and I want to welcome you all to a world of imagination and wonder! In these pages, you'll discover exciting adventures, magical creatures, and lessons to learn. So, grab your favorite blanket, snuggle up, and let's embark on a journey together through the enchanted lands of Mickey and Minnie.

Are you ready? Let's dive in!

This book chronicles the lives of two children and the enduring love of family and friends. It reminds us that sometimes we don't realize the true value of something until it's gone. Having someone to talk openly with, and someone who listens is a precious gift. It's important not to postpone meaningful conversations, as time can slip away unexpectedly. In today's age of social media, maintaining genuine connections can be challenging.

Dear Kids, cherish the moments with your parents as they grow older. Take the time to listen to their stories and be patient with them, just as they were patient with you when teaching you how to walk.

Dear Parents, your children are growing up fast—make memories with them while you can. You may watch the reels later.

The most cherished journey is always returning home, where happiness finds its roots. Those who have someone waiting for them at home are truly blessed.

Don't dwell on your past, don't worry excessively about your future—live in the moment."

With Love, prayers and wishes.

**Binsy Boban Amal**

# CONTENTS


1. My Brother     13
2. Visiting Cousins     17
3. Minnie's Big Day     22
4. Vacation days with Grandparents     26
5. A fun day with Meeku     37
6. Magical Christmas     43
7. Up to the Mountains     50
8. Spooky Halloween     56
9. Little Surprise     62
10 Masha and Bear's Birthday Bash     68

*" a bond like no other, where laughter is endless
and adventures abound, weaving memories
that last a lifetime……."*

# My Brother

His room is a miniature construction site, with toy cranes, bulldozers, and dump trucks scattered around, each one a part of his imaginary world. Mickey is very reserved; he is captivated by the world of cars and construction vehicles and devotes his hours to playing with his cherished toy trucks.

Minnie, on the other hand, is a creative soul who adores drawing and painting. She would spend hours with her colorful crayons, bringing to life vibrant scenes of nature and fantasy.

Despite their differences, Mickey and Minnie share a special bond. Their days are filled with adventures, both real and imaginary. Their adventures have no bounds. Within the confines of their apartment, they transform into fearless explorers, navigating imaginary jungles in the living room and uncovering hidden treasures beneath the cushions. With toy walkie-talkies in hand, they communicate in hushed tones, strategizing their next move like seasoned military agents on a top-secret mission. Sometimes, they play make-believe as restaurant owners, and chefs, serving up imaginary delicacies from their toy kitchen with a side of laughter. Other times, they enact thrilling scenarios as police officers and thieves, darting through the hallways with boundless energy. And when they need a break from their escapades, they cuddle up together on the couch and watch cartoons, their laughter filling the air as they lose themselves in the colorful world on the screen. Minnie would often follow Mickey around as he plays with his toy cars, her sketchbook in hand, capturing the moments of their

adventures together.

Mickey, though reserved, cared deeply for his sister. He would express his love in his own unique way, with playful nudges and teasing. Minnie understood his gestures, knowing that beneath his tough exterior, her brother had a heart of gold. Still, she always complains "Mickey doesn't love me."

One sunny morning, as Mickey played with his favorite toy car in the backyard, Minnie skipped over to him, clutching her box of crayons. "Can I play too, Mickey?" she asked, her eyes sparkling with excitement.

Mickey glanced at Minnie, feeling a bit unsure, but seeing the hopeful look on Minnie's face melted his heart. With a small nod, he handed her a toy car.

Together, they embarked on an imaginary adventure, racing their toy cars around the backyard. Minnie's laughter filled the air, and Mickey couldn't help but smile at the sight of his sister having so much fun.

Suddenly, Mickey's car crashed into her car. Minnie burst into laughter, and Mickey, pretending to be annoyed, tackled her with a playful tickle attack.

As they laughed and rolled around on the ground, their laughter echoing through the crisp autumn air, Mickey and Minnie knew that no matter what adventures awaited them, they would always be there for each other, ready to share in the joy of childhood and the magic of sibling love.

*Binsy Boban Amal*

*"As the day unfolded with laughter and games, the
bond with their cousins grew stronger, etching
memories that would last a lifetime."*
*Cousins are childhood playmates
who grow up to be forever friends!*

# Visiting Cousins

Schools were closed!

One bright summer morning, Mickey and Minnie woke up to warm sunlight streaming through their window. The air was already warm, carrying with it the promise of a beautiful day ahead. Excitement bubbled in their hearts as they dressed in their best clothes and packed their bags. Today was the day they were going to visit their cousins in the neighboring town.

Their bags lay open on the floor, waiting to be filled with essentials for the day's adventure. Mickey packed his favorite toy car, unable to resist the urge to share it with his cousins, while Minnie carefully tucked away her sketchbook and a set of colored pencils, knowing she might find inspiration in the new surroundings. They also have their favorite military man toy in hand. Each item they packed held the promise of endless fun and discovery, fueling their anticipation even further.

As they hopped into the car with their parents, Mickey and Minnie chatted eagerly about all the fun things they would do with their cousins. Mickey, with his shy smile and sparkling eyes, couldn't wait to play with his older cousin's collection of action figures, imagining the epic battles and adventures they would embark on together. Meanwhile, Minnie, her eyes wide with anticipation, dreamed of splashing in the swimming pool with her cousins. The image of her cousins carrying her on their shoulders, and playing her favorite hide and seek, filled her with joy and excitement. And she knew that her aunt, with her warm smile and loving heart, would pamper her like a

princess, showering her with affection and treats, making her feel cherished and adored.

After a short drive, they arrived at their cousins' house, greeted by warm hugs, and excited squeals. Mickey's younger cousin, Naethen, with a mischievous grin, wasted no time in whisking him away to his room, eager to show off his prized collection of action figures, while Dion pulled Minnie into a room filled with her favorite crayons and color pencils. He has a few drawings that Minnie made during her previous visit

All four were soon lost in an epic battle between superheroes and villains with each character's move and countermove, the room filled with laughter and excited shouts, as they plotted and strategized their way through the imaginary battlefield. Meanwhile, their *Ammi* (Aunt) bustled around the house, her arms filled with chocolates and snacks for the kids. She moved with effortless grace, her warm smile lighting up the room as she showered her niece and nephew with treats and affection. But it was Minnie, the little one and the only girl among all the boys, who received special attention from her Ammi. With a gentle touch and a loving gaze, she made sure Minnie felt cherished and included her kindness as a comforting presence during the lively chaos.

In the corner of the room, Benji, their English Cocker Spaniel, lay peacefully, observing the loud noise with his wise, brown eyes. Occasionally, he would wag his tail in approval, as if to say he approved of the joyous chaos unfolding around him. The children would pause their game every now and then to pet him, their laughter mingling with his happy barks.

Hours passed swiftly as Mickey and Minnie engaged in games, shared stories, and laughed with their cousins. Later in the day, they all went to the swimming pool, where they splashed and played together with joyful abandon. Mickey even joined a soccer match with their neighbors, his initial shyness fading in the warmth of family and friends.

As the sun began to set and the day came to an end, Mickey and Minnie reluctantly said their goodbyes to their cousins. Although they were sad to leave, their hearts were full of memories of a day filled with laughter and love.

As they drove back home, Mickey and Minnie smiled at each other, knowing that they were lucky to have such wonderful cousins. And as they drifted off to sleep that night, they dreamed of the next time they would see their cousins again, eagerly anticipating the adventures that awaited them.

*Her heart swells with pride as she watches them grow,*
*their laughter echoing through the house*
*like the sweetest melody.*

# Minnie's Big Day

It's 6 a.m. in the morning, and the world is just beginning to wake up.

After three weeks of holidays, schools are reopening today. It's a busy day at the house, with Mom busy packing their favorite snacks, checking school supplies, and getting ready for the new term ahead.

Mickey and Minnie stood at the bus stop, accompanied by their parents, waiting for the school bus to arrive. Mickey, with his backpack slung over his shoulder, looked excited yet nervous for the day ahead. Minnie, her tiny hand tightly clutching her mother's, gazed up at her with wide eyes, feeling a mix of excitement and anxiety about her first day of School.

She is in her red uniform, new Uniform, new school bags, new shoes, both are excited for their first day.

As the sky painted itself in shades of pink and orange, the school bus pulled up to the roadside, its engine rumbling softly. Minnie's heart raced with anticipation as she climbed onto the bus, her eyes scanning the rows of seats, and walked towards Mickey to his seat. With a smile, Mickey patted the seat next to him, and Minnie eagerly took her place, feeling a surge of comfort being by her brother's side. He made sure to give her, her favorite window seat.

Their parents exchanged reassuring smiles as they watched their children board the bus. "They're growing up so fast," Minnie's mom remarked, her eyes misting with pride, a hint of emotion in her voice as she wiped her eyes.

"They'll be fine," said Mickey's dad, placing a reassuring hand on his wife's shoulder. "And they have each other for support and waved hands and flying kisses to their kids."

As the bus rumbled down the road towards the school, Mickey leaned over to Minnie and whispered words of reassurance. "Don't worry, Minnie. School is going to be so much fun! You'll make new friends and learn exciting things." Minnie nodded, her nerves easing with each word of encouragement from her brother.

As the school reached, her brother held her hand and dropped her off at the class marked KG-1G. He said, 'This is your class, don't worry,' then waved her goodbye and rushed to his own class. Her teacher welcomed her warmly into the classroom. The new day was filled with so much fun and excitement.

Throughout the day, Minnie's nerves dissolved as she immersed herself in the excitement of her first day. She reveled in the joy of making new friends and relished the delicious fruits and snacks during break time.

On the way back, Minnie's mouth was full of excitement, eager to tell her brother all about what happened in class. With each mile that passed, she animatedly shared stories of new friends made, exciting lessons learned, and the wonders of her kindergarten classroom. Once they reached home, Breathless, and eager, they launched into animated explanations of their first day in their new classes. Mom, ever patient and attentive, kept both of them in her lap and listened to their stories with as much enthusiasm as a child among them. With a smile that lit up her face, she savored the magic of their stories, her heart swelling with pride and love for her adventurous children.

*Memories bloom, connecting generations
past and present, weaving a timeless quilt of
family heritage.*

# Vacation Days with Grand Parents

Today is the day we fly to our grandparents for a one-month vacation. In fact, it is one month and 7 days. We are so excited to travel with our parents. Due to COVID, it's been two years since we traveled. We are lucky to have all four grandparents. Minnie hasn't seen many of our relatives; her first visit to India was when she was just a month old, returning after 45 days. And this is just her second visit.

Dubai is always a home away from home, but still traveling back to India is always nostalgic. Dad often says. I call him Abba. Abba and Amma are always nostalgic about their childhood and often remark that we haven't experienced such memories.

This time Abba promised to take us through many places, where Abba and Amma were born and brought up, their schools, their old friends, and how they walked.

Amma's house is nearly 250 kilometers away, which takes us at least 7 hours to drive. It's where Ammamma and Appacha live. Amma's place is cold, whereas Abba's place is hot.

I have seen many of their cousins, but I hardly remember any. I am so excited to visit everyone.

We landed at Cochin International Airport. Abba's house is just an hour from here, so we took a taxi home. Mummy and Appappa were eagerly waiting for us. Abba's Ammachi was also here, but she passed away a month after Minnie was born. I remember bits and pieces of her, but Amma always shows us the video, making it easier to remember.

We arrived around teatime, and Mummy made her special *pazhampori* (banana fritters) with tea. Every time I visit, I treasure my toys, so I rush to show them to Minnie. She was so excited to see them and tipped the box over, scattering all the toys. Mummy came up with a plate full of snacks and glasses of milk for us. While playing she fed us with the snacks.

The next morning, we woke up early, and Appappa took us on his scooter to buy milk. Being in Kerala, we always rise early. Everything in Abba's house runs on a strict schedule: breakfast at 7:30 am, lunch at 1 pm, and dinner at 8 pm. There's a morning prayer at 6 am, although Minnie and I usually don't wake up at that hour.

Back at Abba's house, Mummy had prepared a traditional Kerala breakfast of idli, dosa, and coconut chutney. The aroma of ghee filled the air as we sat down together to eat.

Later that day, after breakfast, we were off to visit *Valiya Daddy's* house (Appappa's elder brother). Visiting elders is a custom every time we come to India. His house is just 10 minutes from ours, so Abba took us on the scooter. On our way back, Abba stopped near his school. My eyes were drawn to a small shop that Abba and Amma fondly called *"petti kada"* (street shop), with colorful items hanging from it.

We want to explore them badly. I remembered Abba's stories about buying snacks and toys from such shops during his school days. *Naranga muttayi, inji puli, jeeraka muttayi,* and many more which I cannot recollect the name. But they are all so colorful.

We bought a few *Naranga muttayi* (lemon candy) and two packets of chips. The shopkeeper uncle wrapped the candy in a newspaper. That seemed strange to me, but it's a usual practice.

Abba, Shenith uncle, Lijo Uncle and Ruben uncle studied here together. They are Abba's best friends. We had been to Shenith uncle's wedding last September. However, Lijo Uncle couldn't join as he was in Ireland. Minnie and I had a great time with *Raphael and Raguel* (Ruben uncle's kids).

There was a football on the ground, and Abba kicked it to me, reminiscing his childhood memories on that school ground. We passed by some classrooms; the seating looked quite different from what we have in Dubai. Minnie and I ran through the classrooms.

Abba made a video call with his friends from their 10th-grade classroom.

We headed back to Mummy's home for a delicious Kerala lunch. I love Mummy's curries; they always have a slight sweetness, so there's no need to worry about the spice.

In two days, we'll be going to Amma's house. Ammamma has been calling and asking when we are coming. Visiting Ammamma's house itself feels like a journey—a 7-hour drive that often turns into 10 or 12 hours as we stop at many places along the way.

Our Ammamma has a special knack for keeping me and my sister engaged. She loves playing games with us and is always ready with answers to my tricky questions. Her presence has a magical way of warding off boredom.

Both houses hold equal importance and joy for us.

In the evening, Mummy took us to the yard where we plucked and collected *Jathikka* (nutmeg) and *Adakka* (areca nut) to dry in the sun. Mummy's yard is abundant with fruits like jackfruit, mangoes, rambutan, and *Chambakka* (rose apples).

I'm not particularly fond of fruits, but Amma is helping Minnie pick them.

For city-bred children like us, it was thrilling to roam the grounds every time, picking up fallen fruits and nutmegs, while enjoying the sights and sounds of little birds, butterflies, and insects. However, mosquitoes were the real villains, especially for Minnie—they seemed to bite her everywhere, despite applying repellent.

There were always squirrels running up and down the trees, and we spotted birds like hummingbirds, kingfishers, mynas, sparrows, and many more.

"I want to show Minnie the 'touch-me-not' plant," I exclaimed excitedly.

"Minnie, come here and touch this plant," I called out.

Amma had shown me this plant during our last vacation. Minnie was surprised to see the plant's leaves curling up when touched. We ran around, searching for more 'touch-me-not' plants.

Most evenings were spent outdoors on the swings or roaming the grounds. Sometimes, Appappa or Mummy would teach us to make toys from coconut leaves. It was thrilling for us to successfully create wristwatches, balls, snakes, and even some animals using *Machinga* (baby coconuts)!

A bath in the evening was a must. Mummy used to take us near the well to bathe, followed by prayer and dinner.

After an early dinner, the family would gathers again on the *verandah* (sit-out) to relax. Appappa have a long charu *kasera* (easy chair) where he would lie down, dressed in just a *mundu* (Dhoti). Mummy and Abba sit nearby in their chairs. Amma always sits on the stairs, while Minnie and I play on the porch.

Amma would tease that this is the "gossip time," where Mummy shares the neighborhood stories, and Abba eagerly asks about everyone's whereabouts.

We love to sleep with Mummy, where the beds are placed on the floor and we all sleep together, cozy, and close.

There are always gatherings at Mummy's house or her ancestral home, where *Chachan* (Mummy's elder brother) now stays. Mummy has two sisters and a brother. When they all gather, the house takes on a festive mood with noisy children scrambling around and relaxed mothers catching up on gossip.

It is a lively and joyful atmosphere filled with family warmth and laughter.

*Pidi and Kozhi* (Indian rice dumplings and chicken curry) is a famous dish prepared when everyone gathers. Pidi, a favorite among the local Christian community, dates to almost 50 AD and was traditionally served only to the royal upper class of Kerala. *Akka* (Mummy's sister) explained this to us.

*Perumbavoor Mummy* (Mummy's elder sister) added to that, *"On pidi day, we all wake up early in the morning. Ammachi (Mummy's mom) would mix the dough and give each of us kids a big ball. We sit down in the kitchen, still half-asleep, and roll the dough into small balls. Meanwhile, outside the kitchen, Appachan (Mummy's dad) would start a fire and boil water to cook the dumplings. It's a cherished family tradition."*

As Abba and our other cousins call Perumbavoor Mummy, we also refer to her the same way, as it signifies the place where she lives. However, Minnie's tongue often slips, and she ends up calling her "Pazhampori Mummy," because every time we visit, she always makes delicious *pazhampori* (banana fritters) for us to enjoy. It has become a playful nickname.

I remember Amma mentioning how this tradition of making pidi was new to her when she got married, as it wasn't practiced in her hometown. Kerala is rich in traditions, and each region has its own unique customs and culinary delights.

And it's heartwarming that even after Ammachi and Appachan have passed away, the next generation continues this tradition. I hope that Minnie and I will also carry it forward one day.

This year holds another special significance for us. Our house is the *tharavad* (ancestral residence) of Appappa, a 70-year-old home built by his father. Now, it's time to demolish it and build a new house. This will be our last vacation in this cherished home. Amma, having come to this house after marriage, holds a deep attachment to it and opposes its demolition. She describes it as cozy, with interconnected rooms and clay roofs that keep it cool inside—a house beloved by everyone.

Outside the house, there is a lawn area with a majestic teak tree and a rambutan tree, with a swing tied to it—a place where we have spent countless hours making memories.

Amma recalls that her family agreed to the marriage only upon seeing this house. However, over time, it has developed leaks during the rainy season, and repairing it no longer suffices. So, reluctantly, we have come to accept the inevitable.

Before bidding farewell to the house, we gathered with Appappa's extended family for a heartfelt get-together. Appappa's siblings were emotional, especially *Valiya Ammayi* (Appappa's sister), who was born and raised in this house. Together, we took photographs in front of the house, enjoyed delicious food, and played with all our cousins.

We started our journey to Ammamma's home at 5 am, with Minnie and me half asleep and clutching our pillows in the back seat for comfort. Our first pitstop was at Trissur Saravanabhavan for breakfast, where the masala dosa is renowned.

Throughout the journey, we made multiple stopovers, but the highlight was lunch at Thamarsherry White House for their famous Mandi biriyani which is our must place to visit every year. The cool breeze had already set in as we navigated the hairpin bends—a drastic change in climate from where we started. We arrived at Ammamma's home around 5 pm.

Ammamma is always well-prepared for our arrival, stocking the pantry with our favorite chips, biscuits, and various homemade snacks, sweets, and savories—all securely stored in locked cupboards. Her Ariyunda, Achappam, and Neyyappam are especially famous.

I believe Amma inherited her culinary passion from

Ammamma.

I'm sure that tonight's dinner will be her famous biriyani. Even if she knows that we arrive late, she'll have it prepared in the afternoon so that she can serve us as soon as we get there.

Appacha runs a bike service center, while Ammamma operates a stitching shop. Amma always brings a bundle of clothes to be stitched there. As Appacha is sick, Ammamma takes care of everything. Days passed quickly as we visited Amma's cousins, her grandmother Ammachi, and a few nearby places.

We have also visited Amma's school, where Ammamma used to be a teacher too. Unfortunately, Ammamma had to quit once Appacha met with an accident. While Amma and Ammamma caught up with their old teachers, Minnie and I played in the school playground.

Soon, it is time to return to Mummy's home.

Usually, on our way back, we take a detour. This time, we're traveling through Ooty, Palakkad, and then to Kochi.

After bidding farewell to Ammamma's home, we started on our return journey. Ammamma made sure to pack some snacks for the road trip. The winding roads of Ooty greeted us with misty mornings and lush greenery that stretched as far as the eye could see. Minnie and I were thrilled by the cool breeze and to experience the heavy fog on the way. We decided to stay for a day to soak in the serene beauty of the hills.

From Ooty, we continued our journey to Palakkad, Abba's friend Vipin Uncle, Sunitha Aunty, and their daughter Mia joined us in Palakkad. Vipin Uncle had worked with Abba in Dubai before relocating to Bangalore, and he remains very close to Abba. We had a wonderful time with them, especially with Mia. We stayed in the same hotel and enjoyed dinner together. Early the next morning, we visited Kalpathy, a beautiful Brahmin settlement that Amma had always wanted to explore. The

place was truly stunning, with its traditional architecture and serene atmosphere. After breakfast, we dispersed to continue our separate plans. We spent another day exploring the local culture and cuisine, especially the viral place Kollangode and viral food the Rawuthar Biriyani. The spicy snacks and delicious dishes of Palakkad left a lasting impression on our taste buds.

By the time we reached Kochi, the familiar sights and sounds welcomed us back. Mummy's home awaited us with open arms, ready to envelop us in its warmth and comfort after our enriching journey visiting Ammamma's home.

In a few days, we are heading back to Dubai. Our schools have already started, so we'll be missing a week of classes. Amma and Abba always prefer to pack on the last day, unwilling to think about leaving. Appappa has already begun organizing things; Mummy is scraping coconut and packing, while Appappa refills coconut oil and stocks up on essentials like chili powder and spices for the kitchen. We assist Valiya Ammayi in gathering vegetables from our yard, ensuring curry leaves are included. Bananas are the last things we pack because they help fill up any leftover space and weight.

At the same time, we're also preparing for Mummy and Appappa's move to a nearby rented house while our new home is being built. We need to shift belongings before our departure. Abba often gets emotional during the final days of our vacation.

It's a bit sad to think about leaving this cozy place where we've made so many memories, but we're also excited to see our friends back in Dubai and to start school again.

As the days pass, we spend our evenings together, enjoying the last moments with our family in Kerala. Mummy prepares delicious meals using ingredients from our yard, and we all sit together on the verandah, sharing stories and laughter.

As the Uber drove away, I saw a tear fall from Mummy's eye, and Abba kept looking back at the home.

Yes, for sure, we will all miss this Tharavadu.

*Home is not just a place; it's where love resides, memories are created, and laughter never ends.*

# A Fun day with Meekhu

Meeku is the little ray of sunshine that brightens up our days. As the youngest among all our cousins, she eagerly awaits the weekends, counting down the days until she can visit us.

While my parents often talk fondly about the days when their home was filled with numerous cousins and relatives, living abroad means that we have fewer family members nearby. However, we are fortunate to have our three cousins close by, and Meeku, the smallest among all of us, her arrival always fills our home with joy and excitement.

Meeku is truly a delight to be around. With her cherubic face and infectious giggles, she brings endless joy to our lives. She has just started speaking, and it's heartwarming to listen to her adorable babble as she tries to imitate everything that my sister, Minnie, and I do.

Meeku's mom, *Aachi*, my favorite aunt, is a constant source of laughter and warmth in our home. She effortlessly blends in with us, treating us as equals and always bringing a sense of fun and playfulness wherever she goes. With her bag filled with cute pencils and funky school supplies, she never fails to delight us with small surprises. My Amma often remarks on the special bond between my Abba and *Aachi* (his sister), and she hopes that Minnie and I will share the same bond as we grow older.

Today is a special day as Meeku is coming to visit. We've planned an outing to the nearby zoo, and we can hardly control our excitement. Minnie and I wait eagerly on the ground floor, peeking out for any sign of Meeku's arrival. When *Chopappa's*

Binsy Boban Amal

(Meeku's dad) car pulls up, we can see Meeku bouncing with excitement as she steps out of the car. Without hesitation, I scooped her up into my arms and rushed inside to begin our day of fun.

We've prepared a surprise for Meeku—a Pink Barbie doll that we know she'll love, pink is her favorite color, Meanwhile, mom bought her favorite chips and candies. As we present her with the gifts, her eyes light up with joy, Playing with Meeku and Minnie may sometimes make me feel like a girl kid, but the laughter and joy we share are worth every moment.

With Meeku's arrival, our home is transformed into a playground of endless adventures. We start on our first escapade of the day - constructing a grand castle out of pillows and bedspreads. Meeku, with her tiny hands and boundless enthusiasm, eagerly pitches in, her laughter filling the room as we work together to bring our fortress to life.

Chopappa is really fun to play with. He used to play all sorts of games with me when I was little. Now that he has a bad back, Amma says we shouldn't play rough games anymore. So, we mostly play chess together now. He is my only companion to play chess, and Abba sometimes, Amma says that's the most boring game.

Amma calls for lunchtime. Whenever Aachi is here, she feeds us all the food on one big plate. She knows just what to feed to fill us up and make our tummies happy.

During lunch, Aachi always has a knack for storytelling, and we eagerly await her next tale as we sit together on the living room floor.

"Once upon a time," she begins, her voice carrying a soothing melody, "there was a magical forest where the trees whispered secrets to the wind..."

As she crafts her enchanting tale, Meeku and I listen with wide-eyed wonder, imagining we are in the middle of this magical forest, encountering all sorts of fantastical creatures. Suddenly, a loud crash interrupts her storytelling. It is Minnie, who knocked over our pillow castle. We all burst into laughter and roll over Minnie.

After a delicious lunch prepared by Amma, we are fueled up and ready for our next adventure: a trip to the zoo. Meeku sticks close to us and insists on sitting in the middle during the car ride. Chopappa left, as he had some work outside. So, it's just Amma, Aachi, and we three kids.

As we arrive at the zoo gates, Amma gives me money to get tickets for all of us, as she says that I'm a big boy now. As we go inside, Meeku, bounces with excitement, her tiny hand clasps tightly in mine as we make our way through the entrance.

Our first stop is the lion's cage, where majestic lions sleep tired in the sun, their golden coats shimmering in the light. Meeku's eyes sparkle with delight as she points to each lion, and shouts, "Look, look!"

Next, we move to the monkey exhibit, where mischievous monkeys swing from branch to branch, their actions entertaining us for hours. Meeku giggles with glee as she watches the playful varieties of monkeys, her laughter echoing through the air. Amma's voice rang in our ears, sternly reminding us not to tease the animals.

Afterward, Amma treats us with ice cream, cooling us down on the warm day. As we explore the zoo further, we encounter a variety of animals, from towering giraffes to graceful zebras. Meeku and Minnie marvel at each new discovery, her curiosity at the sights and sounds of the animal kingdom. As time passes, we sit at a café inside the zoo to have some snacks.

But the highlight of our day comes when we see the elephant near a pond. Meeku is in wonder as she beheld the majestic creatures, their gentle demeanor captivating her heart. With awe-filled expressions, we watch the elephants trumpet and splash in the water, their immense size and grace leaving us spellbound. We even had the chance to climb upon one of the elephants for a short ride.

The time is almost up, it is time to say goodbye to these great creatures of GOD. Sometimes It feels sad to be in the zoo because they had to stay in their cages in the hot sun.

As we go back home, Meeku and Minnie sleep off as they are tired of walking long. They work up as we reach home and start our games again. We're thrilled that Aachi agrees to stay one more day, so we excitedly start planning for tomorrow.

*Through laughter and tales of old, we glimpse a time when
the warmth of togetherness and the simplicity of sharing
brought the true spirit of the season to life.*

# Magical Christmas

Jingle Bells, Jingle Bells!

It's the festive season, the best time of the year. The scent of baking fills the house. Amma soaked the dried fruits three months ago to bake her special plum cake for our friends and relatives. It's a tradition to give cakes to loved ones.

This year, Amma promised to bake cookies and make a gingerbread house too. We're excited because she said we could help. Usually, she won't allow us to be anywhere nearby. Minnie likes to eat the dough. Amma always gives us the last bit of cake batter to lick. It tastes better than the cake itself.

Minnie doesn't like spicy cake with nuts, so Amma makes a plain one for her (and us). She puts the icing on it too. Amma talks about the old sugar icing *Ammamma (*Grandma) used to make.

The homemade wine is ready to be bottled. Amma always prepares it at least three months in advance. Abba is currently filling the bottles. The Christmas trees have already been decorated. Amma warned Minnie not to touch them, threatening that Christmas would be canceled next year if she did.

This year, it's a silver and red theme. We try to make every year special. We are going to decorate the house. Abba brought all the boxes from the garage which is filled with previous year's decoration items.

Even though we have everything here, Amma and Abba say they miss the Christmas vibe back home and their childhood memories.

I visited Kerala for Christmas. I enjoyed the unique carols

*Binsy Boban Amal*

there—they're different from what I'm used to. Ammamma and Mummy's special dishes, although spicy and tangy, are absolutely delicious. They no longer bakes cakes; instead, we buy them, and relatives also bring cakes over. During Christmas in India, all my cousins gather at one house. I've witnessed Ammamma killing a hen for lunch. Apppappa used to take us to buy meat in his scooter, and I recall seeing a poor buffalo and goat there.

Amma always has her childhood stories to tell. "Life wasn't like this when we were young," she says all the time. This time, Amma started recounting her Christmas memories. I've heard it many times before, but it's always nice to hear it again, especially for Minnie.

*"It all begins with preparing wine at least three months in advance. Ammamma makes wine using whatever seasonal fruit is available. The 25 days of Lent start on the 1st of December, but we kids only start observing the last week before Christmas. Appacha would construct the Christmas tree on the lawn, fashioning it from branches. It was a real tree, not artificial like they are now."*

A real Christmas tree?

Minnie interrupted Amma with many questions, she was confused, how is the Christmas tree a real tree?

Amma patiently answered all our questions. *We, the kids, would start making decorations. Unlike now, we don't have many things available on the market. We reused items from the previous year and bought some colored paper. The rest we made ourselves. We hung ice cream bowls and last year's Christmas cards on the tree along with any beautiful small toys or dolls we could find.*

"A Christmas Card? "

Minnie asked about Christmas cards with excitement. Amma explained that in those days, we used to buy many Christmas cards from the shop. Since we didn't have phones or WhatsApp, we would send cards by post or give them directly to our loved ones. Sometimes, we even made cards ourselves using chart paper, paper cutting, and glitter pens.

*"All the kids would try to be creative," Amma said. These paper items would melt in the foggy mornings. So, we hung most items on the last few days when Santa came home.*

*"We had a 10-day holiday for Christmas," Amma continued. "But before that, we had Christmas exams at school. The last day of the exam was the Christmas celebration. We could wear colorful dresses, make a tree, and exchange Christmas cards. There was also a custom called Christmas friend."*

"A Christmas Friend?"

Another one from Minnie. She thought it was a special friend for Christmas.

*Amma explained that they used to write all the names on pieces of paper, and each person would pick a name. That person would become their Christmas friend, and they would keep the name a secret. On the day of exchanging gifts, everyone would bring a present for the friend whose name they had picked.*

*"In class, we'd play pranks on that friend," Amma said.*

*"The 10 days of holidays were truly wonderful," Amma continued. "Your Ammamma would begin baking cakes. She was a remarkable chef, known for her delectable cakes and delicious dishes. Although she doesn't bake as often now, her biryani remains a cherished specialty within our family."*

Minnie interrupted, "Amma, finish the Christmas story, then start the biryani story."

Everyone laughed.

*"In the final five days, carols would begin arriving from various churches," Amma recounted. "I was always frightened by Santa's drumming. On Christmas Eve, we would attend church. The weather was bitterly cold; us children often fell*

*asleep before midnight."*

" *On Christmas day, the whole family would gather in one home," Amma continued. "Your Appacha (Grandpa) always made sure to bring everyone together. He was a true family person who strengthened our bonds. All of us played outside while Aunties cooked, and uncles enjoyed chit chats. Since there were no WhatsApp or mobile phones, everyone gathered and talked about anything and everything.*

" *There was no Netflix or any online platforms back then, " Amma said. "New movie releases were aired on TV only on special festive days. We all gathered in front of the TV after a hearty feast to watch the new movie.*

*Appacha used to buy plenty of firecrackers for all of us.*

Some mistakes never fade from our memory. One Christmas Eve, I recall vividly when Amma's brother, who lives far away, surprised us on the afternoon of December 24th. He invited me and my sister to come to Amma's home to stay and enjoy the festivities. All our cousins were there, and I eagerly agreed to go with them. My sister, being more mature, initially refused, but under pressure from everyone, she reluctantly joined us.

On our way to Amma's home, we stopped at Appacha's shop. We told him we were heading to Amma's with our uncle, and he nodded, handing over a packet of crackers wrapped in newspaper. Excitedly, I took them, and we continued to Amma's home where we had a wonderful time with our cousins, while my sister looked sad. As a child, I didn't understand why she was sad.

Years later, I realized that Abba had bought those crackers to celebrate Christmas at home with us. We had chosen spending time in our cousins' company over spending the holiday with our parents, unknowingly leaving behind our father's festive plans. While my parents may have forgotten this incident, it remains a scar on my heart.

Abba screamed, "Check the cake, something is burning."

While Amma rushed to the oven, Minnie whispered in my ears, "I think Amma is lying; it's a made-up story."

We both burst into laughter and ran to play.

While in the yard, I noticed Amma resting her head on Abba's shoulder.

......Maybe she's missing Appacha.

*Nothing compares to a friend with whom you can be yourself, sharing all your silly and mischievous thoughts. Friends create memories with you, support your wild decisions, and still watch out for you.*

# Up to the Mountains

I could hear Amma screaming... yes, I know the reason, I haven't packed yet.

Minnie is relaxed; she hasn't decided what to wear yet. She won't like what Amma asked her to wear; she always prefers her own choice.

Today, we're heading out for camping. In the Middle East, we only get a few months of winter, so camping becomes our main activity during this time. It's going to be busy since it's the weekend, and we need to arrive early to secure a good spot. A few weeks ago, we went camping for my cousin's birthday, but this time we're joining Joshu and his family. Joshu is my friend, and our parents were friends even before he was born. They'll be here soon, but we're still packing.

*There is a story behind Amma's and Aunty's friendship. They refer to themselves as 'valapottukal,' like broken bangles that are kept safe even if broken. They also call themselves 'roadside friends.' After moving to Dubai. Amma went for an interview where Tara Aunty was also present. With her blah blah blah behavior, Aunty struck up a conversation with Amma and, in the end, asked if Abba could drop her home as she was new to the area. That marked the beginning of their friendship, which has continued as family friends for 10 years and counting.*

Abba is helping Amma pack; the things we have packed make it seem like we are going on vacation, but it's just for a one-night stay.

As we sleep inside the tent on the mountain, we make sure

to take whatever thick blankets or bed sheets are available at home to lay on the floor as our bed. Our air bed is broken, so we use these items to create our bed. Warm clothes and blankets are necessary because it will be cold in the mountains.

I packed my toys, like the scoops and bucket from the beach toys and the construction toys so that we can dig and play there.

Amma and Thara Aunty are on speakerphone, going through their checklist. "You take that… I take this…" That's all I could understand.


We will be doing barbeque, so Amma already marinated chicken in the morning and put it in the freezer,

Abba is doing the last check.

Oil,

Frying pan

Bread

Egg

Spoons

Water can

Omg…. That's a huge list…

Minnie jumped up when she heard the word "egg". She loves eggs so much that she would eat all six if you gave them to her in a day.

Looking at her excitement, Amma told us, "Eggs and bread are for breakfast. You are not allowed to ask for dinner." That's a slight disappointment for Minnie, although it's a ray of hope that she gets in the morning.

Jobin Uncle called; they would be here any minute. We are heading towards the parking. We are planning to go in one car if everything fits. It will be a fun 2-hour drive.

Abba and Uncle somehow managed to fit everything into their KIA Carrens. It's a bit congested, but everyone adjusted to fit in. It was a 2-hour journey, and we started playing *rock paper scissors* inside the car.

As we arrived around sunset, the sky painted in hues of orange and purple welcomed us to our camping spot on the mountain. Despite the cramped car ride, excitement filled the air as we quickly unloaded and set up at our campsite.

Abba and Uncle efficiently unpacked the car while Amma and Thara Aunty organized the cooking supplies.

Minnie, still buzzing with energy, ran around exploring the area with Joshu, picking up sticks and rocks along the way. I helped Abba assemble the tent.

While we played around, the aroma of Amma's marinated chicken filled the air as she prepared the barbecue. Amma handed us the juices as we played.

There were lots of other families around; some played music loudly, and others were dancing. Some families gathered around bonfires, while others were busy setting up tents or preparing meals. The atmosphere was lively and festive, with children running around and laughter filling the air. We joined a group of kids playing 'tag' nearby, Minnie's giggles blending with the sounds of nature and distant music. As the evening wore on, families started to wind down, gathering around their own campfires to share stories and roast marshmallows under the starlit sky.

Abba and uncle washed us and changed our dress as we were covered in dust.

We gathered around our table to enjoy the grilled chicken, *kuboos* (Arabic bread), and *hummus* (dip).

After dinner we gathered around our folding table, playing cards by streetlight and sharing stories and laughter under the starlit sky. Amma handed out snacks and drinks, and Minnie's face lit up with joy as she participated in our card games.

After changing our clothes because we were covered in dust, we couldn't play in the dust again, so we played Monopoly, Snake and Ladder, and many more games.

As it was getting colder, we moved to our tents.

Our cozy blankets and beds made from blankets and sheets kept us warm from the cold mountain air.

The next morning, we woke up to the crisp mountain air and the smell of eggs and bread cooking over the portable stove.

We brushed our teeth and rushed to play. While Joshu and I started playing, Minnie eagerly helped Amma with breakfast (just for the eggs), her disappointment from the night before forgotten in the excitement of a new day of adventure. Before the sun hit hard, we packed up our campsite, leaving no trace behind, and headed back home with memories of a weekend filled with laughter, good food, and the beauty of nature.

55

*Underneath the flickering jack-o'-lanterns and amid
laughter echoing through the neighborhood, we found magic
in costumes, crafts, and the warmth of community,
along with the cherished love of our cousins.*

# Spooky Halloween

Today we are very excited. Our first ever Halloween party !!.. Hurray..

It's being hosted at our cousin's place, who lives in a community with twenty families.

Dion, our Beda Achacha, and Naethen, our chota Achacha, they are our all-time favorites.

Abba dropped me and Minnie early afternoon, with Amma and Abba set to join us later in the evening.

By the time we arrived, all the kids in the community had already started the preparation for Halloween.

Some were busy carving pumpkins, others were fixing lanterns, and a few were crafting ghost and spider webs. We eagerly joined in with our handful of craft items, ready to add our own spooky decorations to the mix.

We gathered on the car porch of Villa No. 4 to escape the heat, where *Ammi* (our Aunt) treated us with refreshing orange juices and snacks. Ammi, being artistic herself, shared some of her creative ideas and joined us in crafting decorations. Meanwhile, other kids around Minnie's age were busy under the guidance of other Aunts, decorating baskets for the festivities.

*Illippa* (Achacha's dad) and other uncles were busy adorning the houses, car porches, and pathways with decorations, creating a festive atmosphere that was both spooky and inviting.

As the sun began to set, casting long shadows across the neighborhood, the excitement for our Halloween party grew

even more. The decorations were coming together beautifully, thanks to everyone's efforts. Illippa and the others had transformed the houses with cobwebs, eerie lights, and even some friendly ghost figures that swayed in the breeze.

Ammi, with her keen eye for detail, helped us assemble miniature haunted houses out of cardboard and painted them with glowing windows and bats hanging from the eaves. She even showed us how to make ghostly shapes out of tissue paper that we could hang in the trees outside.

As dusk settled in, the neighborhood began to come alive with the sounds of laughter and excitement. The adults lit jack-o'-lanterns and placed them strategically along the pathways, creating a path of flickering orange light that led up to each house.

It's time for the costume change for the trick-or-treat. All the kids went back to their respective houses to dress up.

Beda Achacha had meticulously carved his pumpkin to resemble a famous lightning-shaped scar and glasses, turning himself into a recognizable Harry Potter. Chota Achacha, with a mischievous grin, donned a magician's cape and top hat, ready to perform tricks that would leave us all amazed.

Minnie, with her love for animals, decided to dress up as a sleek black cat. Ammi had painted her face with whiskers and adorned her costume with a fluffy tail and ears. It was adorable and perfectly suited her playful personality.

As for me, inspired by the spooky decorations around us, I chose to dress as a friendly ghost. With a white sheet draped over me and eye holes cut out.

Ammi is now the official face painter, and every kid gathered around her to have spooky designs painted on their faces.

Among the other neighborhood kids, there was Ayesha, who had transformed herself into a friendly witch with a pointed hat and broomstick.

Next to Ayesha was Gagan, dressed as a spooky skeleton with glowing bones painted on his black outfit.

At the craft table, Nikunj and Appu were diligently working on their own creations. Paaru, dressed as a shimmering fairy with glittering wings, was adding sparkly touches to her enchanted wand. Raami, in his homemade zombie costume with torn clothes and painted scars.

With Amma and Abba arriving soon, the party was about to kick into high gear. The scent of hot cider and cinnamon wafted through the air, and someone had set up a spooky music playlist that added to the ambiance.

As the sun dipped below the horizon, casting long shadows across the neighborhood, all the kids gathered excitedly in front of Villa No. 1 sharp at 6:30 pm. We were adorned in our elaborate costumes, clutching lantern baskets filled with candies and costume accessories. With eager anticipation, we began our Halloween tradition of trick-or-treat. We moved from house to house, knocking on doors adorned with spooky decorations. Each time the door creaked open, we greeted the neighbors with cheerful chants of "Trick or treat!" The thrill was in receiving treats—delicious chocolates, colorful candies, and even homemade snacks from some creative parents.

Soon, the streets echoed with laughter and playful banter as we compared our loot and swapped candies. The best part was discovering which houses had the most treasured treats, sparking friendly competition among us.

As the night progressed, all the parents emerged from their homes, dressed in mysterious black attire, and gathered around a table laden with an array of Halloween-themed snacks. Amma and Aunt Ammi had worked their magic in the kitchen, creating spooky crackers shaped like ghosts and witches' hats. Other treats included creepy cupcakes with edible spider webs, bowls of gooey, green slime jelly, spooky eyeball tacos, deadly crackers, and many more.

We were all eager to taste everything and circled the table like little ghosts and goblins. There were contests announced for the best creative Halloween food and the most impressive costumes. Everyone eagerly awaited the results, each hoping to win a prize for their efforts.

The evening continued with lively chatter and excitement, as we recounted our adventures from the night's trick-or-treating and admired each other's costumes. As the night drew to a close, we gathered for a final group photo on the porch of Villa No. 4, everyone proudly displaying their handmade crafts and wearing smiles that stretched from ear to ear. It was a Halloween party we would never forget, filled with family, friends, and memories that would last a lifetime.

*Even a small act of bravery can bring the brightest smiles.
Love and laughter always find a way to mend our hearts
and create cherished memories.*

# Little Surprise

Minnie was very cranky today as her favorite doll is broken. She was deeply attached to that doll.

They had tea parties together and read bedtime stories. But now, the doll's head hangs loosely, and its eyes aren't bright anymore. Minnie tried to fix it with some buttons, but it still looked sad. She sat in her room feeling sad.

I saw how sad Minnie was. I quietly left to find something to make her feel better. I wanted to see her smile again. I asked Amma if she could stitch and fix the doll's head at least.

Amma was busy in the kitchen and said, yes, "Maybe later." I felt bad. Even though I sometimes fight with Minnie, I can't see her being sad. So, I took the sewing kit and tried to fix it myself. But then, Oouch…accidentally, the needle pricked my finger and a drop of blood appeared.

Oops!!!

Minnie screamed when she saw the blood, and Amma rushed into the room.

I was worried that Amma would scold me.

But to my surprise, she patiently looked at my finger and seemed worried.

*Amma, "I'm Sorry! I thought I could fix it for Minnie so that she would feel happy "I explained.*

She kissed me on my forehead and hugged me, Jealous Minnie jumped over us as she saw Amma hugging me. We rolled over to the bed and she is happy now.

Amma always smiles when we play together and now, she is fixing Minnie's doll.

Soon I saw her checking something on the phone and announced to us that tomorrow we had a surprise.

Our eyes widened with excitement! We eagerly asked her.

Surprise is surprise!! Amma teased us.

That's a disappointment. Still waiting is exciting.

Minnie leaned in close to Amma, asking eagerly, "Is it a new doll? Or a new toy?"

Finally, she revealed "We are going for a movie tomorrow "A 3D movie.

We were surprised and intrigued.

A 3D Movie?? Minnie asked with curiosity.

I have heard about it, but Minnie, it's her first-time hearing about it.

Amma nodded and said, *"Yes, a 3D movie is different from the usual movies. It's something you have to experience to understand."*

Minnie turned to me, I said, I am not sure. But I have heard that it's a movie where we get sunglass."

Sunglasses? She is not convinced.

"I'm not sure," I admitted. "But I heard that's part of it. We'll find out tomorrow.

Excitement filled the air as we imagined what the 3D movie experience would be like. Tomorrow couldn't come soon enough!

The next day, we woke up early, feeling excited about our surprise movie day. The movie is at 11 am Amma packed a small bag with snacks, our favorite candies, and some water to enjoy during the movie. We couldn't wait to see "Avatar 2" in 3D!

Arriving at the movie theater, we saw the big posters and many people around buying tickets and snacks. Amma led us to the theater showing "Avatar 2" in 3D. We got our special 3D glasses and found our seats, ready for the adventure to begin.

Minnie is so delighted that she got new glasses.

As the lights dimmed and the movie started, we put on our glasses and were instantly transported to the world of Pandora. The 3D effects were incredible! We felt like we were flying with the characters and exploring the magical forests and mountains right alongside them. Minnie was scared and screamed initially when the Avatar was flying towards her. We all laughed.

Amma explained the difference and put her in Amma's lap. But she got very excited and then sat in her seat.

During the exciting parts of the movie, we held onto our seats and gasped in awe. The 3D glasses made everything seem so real and close to us.

Halfway through the movie, there was an interval. Amma took out the snacks that we brought from home, and she also bought us caramel popcorn and juice from the theater. We happily munched on the snacks and candies while discussing our favorite scenes so far. It was fun to take a break and chat about all the amazing things we had seen. Amma also explained to us about "Avatar 1" which was released when Amma was in college.

As there were fewer people in the theater for the movie, Minnie was running around between the seats.

When the movie resumed, we were even more excited to see what would happen next. The adventure continued with more thrilling moments and surprises that kept us glued to our seats until the very end.

As the credits rolled and the lights came back on, we sat there for a moment, still amazed by everything we had experienced. Amma asked us how we liked the movie, and we both exclaimed, "It was awesome!"

Minnie was so eager and asked, 'When will Avatar 3 come?' We all laughed.

Now she wants to see more 3D movies, and so do I.

*"I'm so glad you enjoyed it,"* Amma said with a smile. "

Leaving the theater, we chatted excitedly about our favorite parts of the movie and how much fun we had together.

We couldn't wait to tell Abba all about our 3D movie adventure when we got home.

*A day adorned with love, laughter, and the simple delights of childhood. Each moment, each smile, each gift wrapped with care—these are the memories that will forever linger in our hearts.*

# Mash and Bear Birthday

Our little one is turning four this Tuesday. I can't believe how fast time has flown by—it feels like just yesterday that we welcomed her into our lives.

She is a pure gem. My amma used to say, 'Kids are like two eyes, we cannot say which is more important or which one we love more.' Before having them, I never truly understood that sentiment. But after Mickey and Minnie were born, I felt it deeply—I became so emotional. Both of them are my precious gems. I know it's the same for all parents.

We couldn't celebrate her last birthday due to Covid, so this year she wanted it to be extra special. She asked for a Masha and Bear cake.

I wanted to make this birthday special for her, something she'll always remember. My Amma used to bake cakes herself for all my birthdays, decorating them with her own designs on top with sugar icing. Those memories are deeply cherished by me—the smell and taste of butter, especially homemade butter, made those cakes so special.

She carefully collects the cream from boiled milk, and once the bottle is full, she will make butter from it.

Why shouldn't I create the same memories for my daughter?

This year I have planned to bake a cake for my daughter and make her birthday memorable.

Mickey is just as excited. Last year, we threw him a Mario-themed birthday party where he dressed up as Mario and Minnie as Luigi. We decorated the house with Mario-themed decorations and had a Mario cake, and it was a huge hit with everyone.

With Mickey's Mario-themed birthday party still fresh in our memories as a big success, I'm putting all my creativity into planning a special Masha and the Bear birthday celebration for our little princess. I've been busy researching decoration ideas, sketching out cake designs, and thinking of fun activities that will make her day unforgettable. Minnie's Abba is my full-time support, even though he is nowhere to be seen.

Mickey is eager to help too. He's been suggesting ideas for games and even volunteered to dress up as Bear to surprise his sister. It warms my heart to see their excitement and how they support each other.

I'm not a "pro" baker or even a home baker, but there's something special about putting effort into something homemade. Kids always love beautifully decorated cakes, but they truly appreciate the effort once they're older to realize. I often find myself missing my Amma's cakes and those cherished days now.

Those days, my Amma and *Sheela Aunty* (my Appa's sister) were the expert bakers in our family. Even though they used the same recipe, Amma's cakes always turned out white while Aunty's were always brown. It was a big mystery and topic of conversation back then.

Nowadays, only Shyni Aunty (my aunt) makes cakes. Whenever we visit India, she prepares a variety of sweets. She truly enjoys experimenting with different recipes.

We should truly call our older generation geniuses. They lived, learned, and cooked without YouTube or Instagram.

I still cherish a recipe book handwritten by Amma, which she gave me before I moved to Dubai. There's also a green-covered book that she tucked into my luggage when I moved to my in-laws' house after my wedding. These items hold precious memories and recipes that remind me of her love and care.

In today's world where we can find recipes instantly online,

I often think about how our elders learned to cook through experience, intuition, and a deep understanding of flavors. They shared their knowledge not through screens or social media, but through personal connections and moments spent together.

As I get ready to bake a special cake for my daughter's birthday, I feel thankful for the traditions and skills passed down to me. These recipe books are not just about cooking; they are a legacy of love, creativity, and family bonds that I want to pass on to Mickey and Minnie as they grow up, just like my Amma did for me.

Actually, my Amma used to stitch my birthday dresses as well. Somehow, I didn't inherit her sewing skills—my sister did. So, I asked my tailor to custom-make a Masha dress for my daughter instead. It's a pink pinafore with a white top underneath and a small scarf as an accessory.

We bought a Masha and Bear soft toy to use as decoration. This time, we decided to organize it as a playdate for Masha. We set up a picnic mat on the floor and decorated it with picnic baskets, fruits, cookies, and donuts.

For the cake, we kept it simple and made her favorite strawberry cake with pink frosting and a Masha decoration on top. It was my first time working with fondant, and I was pleased with how it turned out.

Minnie was thrilled when she saw the cake. Her happiness made all the effort worthwhile.

As always, Minnie's favorite Beda Achacha and Chotta Achacha arrived, followed by Minnie's little sister, Meeku, and their parents too.

This time, the celebration was even more special because Minnie's favorite extended cousins—Malu Chechy, Minnu Chechy, and Appu—joined the fun as well.

Everyone arrived with hands full of gifts for Minnie. She was eager to open them all right away, but I had already told her that we would open the gifts last, after everyone had left. Minnie, being a smart girl, carefully stored all the gifts away.

Since it was Minnie's birthday, Mickey also received some gifts as a bonus. Minnie excitedly showed her little sister Meeku all the decorations and explained everything to her.

Aachi and Ammi, her favorite aunts, along with Valiyamma and Anju Mummy, showered Minnie with hugs and kisses, making her feel truly special on her big day. Even though Appu is just two months younger than Minnie, she feels like a big sister to him. Appu and Meeku were the stars of the show.

The kids all rushed inside to play, and before their dresses could get spoiled, we decided to cut the cake.

I brought the cake out of the fridge, and all the kids started jumping with excitement. We played Minnie's favorite song on the speaker and lit the candles on the cake. As she blew out the candles, a tear escaped from my eye.

*"My little girl... Thank God for everything,"* I whispered quietly to myself.

After cutting the cake and enjoying some messy fun with it, we organized small games for the kids to play. Minnie always gets upset if she loses, but being the birthday star, her Achachas let her win every game. It was heartwarming to see the siblings support and love each other so much.

Kichu, their Beda Achacha, holds a special place in my heart—he's like my first baby. I always tell Mickey that Beda Achacha is Amma's first baby. Dion, AKA Kichu was born just after I completed my degree and started my first job. He was chubby and adorable. Kichu has been a constant source of joy and companionship throughout the years. When he was born, I remember feeling overwhelmed with love and responsibility, much like I did when Mickey and Minnie came into our lives.

I still recall the time when my sister brought me to Dubai

for a visit, just so I could spend time with Kichu. Those ten days were filled with laughter, baby giggles, and a deepening bond between us. Even after I moved to Dubai permanently, Kichu remained a bright spot in my life, always ready with a smile and a mischievous twinkle in his eye.

Now, seeing Kichu playfully interacting with Mickey and Minnie at Minnie's birthday party, I couldn't help to believe he's already 12 years old.

He has grown from that chubby baby into a caring and thoughtful older brother, always ensuring that his younger cousins feel loved and included.

As the kids love noodles, I prepared a Chinese feast today, with a spread of delicious dishes including Hot and Sour soup, Spring rolls, Chicken chow Mein, Fried rice, Chicken Manchurian, and Beef with Broccoli. The aroma of these dishes filled the house, and the kids eagerly gathered around the table, excited to enjoy their favorite Chinese meal together. During any gatherings, I always prefer to cook food at home rather than buy from restaurants.

Mickey helped Abba to serve homemade wine to the adults, while the kids enjoyed homemade watermelon juice. Keeping the kids in one place was a challenge—they were running all over the house with excitement.

After dinner, we gathered to play some games. We started with Anthakshari, where everyone sang songs and had a lot of fun. Then, we played Damsherats, acting out different clues and laughing together at the guesses.

It was a lively evening filled with good food, laughter, and bonding moments with family.

Departure is always sad, it was almost 1 am, and everyone planned to disperse.

As the day unfolded, Minnie's smile never faded. It was a birthday filled with happiness, new memories, and the simple joys of childhood—proof that sometimes, the simplest gestures and homemade delights can create the most unforgettable moments. I felt immense gratitude for my family. They are my pillars of strength, and occasions like these remind me of the blessings that fill our lives each day.

***

9 789359 736303